Life Has Meaning

A Selection of Short Stories and Poetry

Life Has Meaning

A Selection of Short Stories and Poetry

Regina Jenkins Emerson

Triple J Publishing
Sanford

Regina Jenkins Emerson

Life Has Meaning: A Selection of Short Stories and Poetry

Cover Designed by Ophelia W. Livingston
Cover photo iStockphoto®

ISBN-13: 978-0-9840853-5-4
ISBN-10: 0-9840853-5-1

Short Stories and Poetry
Edited by Barbara S. Keller

Triple J Publishing, Sanford, North Carolina
Printed in the United States of America
www.triplejpublishing.com

Library of Congress Control Number: 2011928820

DEDICATION

This book is dedicated to my mother, Dorothy Elaine Lindsey, who was a hardworking treasure: priceless, genuine, and strong. She was addicted to reading; books were her best friend. My love for reading was a natural gift from her.

My mother taught me the importance of not believing everything you hear, but to explore and seek on your own. This became one of the foundations of my love for reading. My mother was a single parent who reared six children with the help of my aunts, uncles, and a whole lot of help from my grandmother. Needless to say, we were poor and most often couldn't afford to vacation, travel or do some of the more elaborate things enjoyed by families who had greater means than our own.

However, I could read about the people and wonderful places outside my little Chatham County, NC world; and somehow, my mother bought me a book every week. I often found myself turning to her after I'd finished a book, and saying, "If I had written that story I would have done it this way or that." She'd always laugh and tell me my way would have sounded better. She meant it from her heart without ever realizing her words would become my encouragement to write.

My mother knew that life has meaning and demonstrated a desire to have a deeper understanding of the meaning of matters related to life. This taught me at an early age to believe in God and to open my mind to new ways of looking at obstacles in my path. Above all else, my mother gave us love, and that was the most important thing of all.

I dedicate this book to my mother because she gave me so much, and she taught me that *life has meaning*.

CONTENTS

ACKNOWLEDGMENTS

My husband James, who is the love of my life; and our children, Nikki and Jamie: You've always supported me in my writing ventures and allowed me the private time to write. You've been very patient over the years and never seemed to think I was ignoring you when I was in my "writing world."

My niece, Chasity Lindsey and my aunt, Brenda Womble: Special thanks for reading my stories and giving me positive criticism, encouragement, and solid advice.

My teachers—the late Mrs. Inease Wicker and the late Mr. John McIntyre; Mr. Jerry Wilson and Mrs. Betty Caviness: You not only taught me, but you also encouraged me to express myself through writing.

Ophelia Livingston, my sorority sister and friend: I owe you everything for your guidance, wisdom and patient ways, and for your help in getting this book published. You are a woman of tremendous knowledge and talents, and I can't thank you enough for sharing them with me.

Barbara Kellcr, my editor: I never knew editing involves so much! Thank you eternally. You're among the best!

Rosa Lindsey, my deceased grandmother, to whom most of the credit for this book is due. Her storytelling was not just a form of entertainment but also a blessing in my life.

Thanks to all who encouraged me to write, write, write!!!

.

INTRODUCTION

When you think about the cares and reasons of life, the thoughts can become very deep. Life is one big story with its beginning, middle, and end. *Life Has Meaning* is Regina Emerson's first publication. It is a collection of short stories and poems about ordinary and extra-ordinary events with natural and unnatural but colorful characters.

It includes a variety of interesting plots that will make your imagination soar from fright to humble love. Some of the stories were inspired by the comings and goings and scenarios of the small town where the author grew up and experienced life. The book includes nine stories and three poems, including:

"Tragedy Among Friends" – the tale of college friends who reunite later in life with a surprising turn of events.

"The Letters" – a lost purse brings two strangers together in an unimaginablc and unforgettable way.

"'Cause Granny Don't Lie" – a frightfully entertaining ghost tale based on a story told to the author by her grandmother.

"Sacred Tale" – a page turner, filled with love, murder, and unexpected consequences.

"A Warm December" – reveals the love between two young people that was almost lost.

"I Consider It Holy" – strange occurrences that can only be described as divine intervention. True believer or unbeliever: you decide.

"He Called Me Daughter" – the strength of a touch.

"My Joe: The Greatest Love Story" – a familiar story but unlike you've ever heard it told.

"Summer of the Deer" – a sad love story, rich with prejudice and the supernatural.

∾⋑⋐∾

Happenings, reasons, and what makes the world go 'round is how *Life Has Meaning* describes what happens on our journey of existence.

ARBITRARY BILLOWING

TRAGEDY AMONG FRIENDS

We had all been friends since college. That's where we all met: Bryant and Nicole, BettyMichelle and Gavin; and my dearest soul mate, Tim, and me. Nicole, BettyMichelle, and I were roommates in Benton Hall at Bell, our fine college in coastal North Carolina. Nicole and BettyMichelle were both from Baltimore and had attended high school together, but the others of us were from different states. Bryant was from Texas, Gavin from Alabama, and Tim was from Iowa. I was from North Carolina, "the good Old North State."

It was 1973 when we fell in love with Bell College and the men we met there. In keeping with a Bell tradition, the college arranged for all the new underclassmen to go to Southport, a nearby seaport town, where we would catch the ferry to Fort Fisher. There the college sponsored an all day cookout as a time for us freshmen to meet and mingle with the folk with whom we would be spending our next four years.

For this occasion, many students drove to Southport; my roommates and I were among them. Nicole and BettyMichelle rode together, but I drove alone. As fate would have it, there was a traffic jam on the main road into Southport.

Those of us hoping to be aboard the ferry could only sit helplessly as the minutes to its departure ticked off our dashboard clocks. By the time we parked and hurried to the ferry terminal, all we could see was the back of the ferry disappearing across the horizon and the wake left in its path. Well, so much for meeting mingling.

As I joined Nicole and BettyMichelle to lament our misfortune, it was obvious we were not alone in this predicament. Besides, what could we do but make the best of this disappointing situation? The answer was staring at us from just a few steps away: three Bell men in the same disappointing situation as we. Our eyes locked, and together we howled in one huge chorus of laughter! We decided to have our own picnic in the ferry terminal area. We could "meet and mingle" after all!

Each fellow sort of chose which of us he wanted to chat with. Tim, just the one I wanted, approached me first. Whoever would have guessed this chance meeting would turn out to be so right!

We started dating that very evening and soon became inseparable.

The six of us, now three inseparable couples, enjoyed each other's company and did almost everything together. We partied together, took some classes together, and went to church together. During one semester break, we even went on a cruise together. Our dates included bowling, movies, sports tournaments, house parties, and much, much more. We had tons of fun, but we took our studies seriously; and on a gloriously beautiful day in the spring of 1977, we all graduated amidst the pomp and pageantry of the occasion and the applause and smiles of our proud families.

We were lucky and favored by God to receive jobs right there in the area of our college. Bryant and Gavin both landed jobs as accountants at the Bank of Southport. Tim became the coach at New Hanover High. We girls all grabbed elementary teaching positions at three of the area schools.

Gavin was a quiet loving fellow from a good family. He was the youngest of three boys. His older brothers were twins. Bryant was fun-loving and engaging but seemed a bit insecure. Tim was an only child who was sent to me from God. He was smart, respectful and proud to have me as his mate.

BettyMichelle was full of fun. She laughed a lot and just enjoyed life. Nicole, however, was just the opposite: often very quiet; sometimes pensive and sometimes withdrawn, but very kind.

We'd worked one year after graduation when we each received an engagement ring as a gift on Christmas Day, 1978. Having done everything together since our freshman year, our marriages just had to be a triple ceremony.

Suddenly, wedding plans became priority in our lives. We girls looked through bridal magazines, visited bridal shops, and planned, planned, planned. Every opportunity we got found us at each other's apartment discussing every detail of our future day of bliss. The guest list was composed over dinner.

Saturdays became the day for caterer appointments and shopping for decorations. But as our wedding day got closer, something with Nicole, we sensed, wasn't quite right. She just didn't seem as excited about wedding plans as BettyMichelle and I. Even during our wedding portrait sittings, Nicole seemed too somber for a soon-to-be bride. BettyMichelle asked her if she were okay, but Nicole never really answered, just responded with her familiar inexplicable smile and a gentle raising and lowering of her shoulders.

Once, when BettyMichelle and I were alone, she—a lot more outspoken that I—had asked if I'd noticed lately that Nicole and Bryant seemed uncomfortable with each other when we were all together. I was glad she'd raised the question. At least I knew what I was thinking wasn't just in my head. BettyMichelle's jokes always had the group doubled over laughing, but lately her jokes were not funny to Bryant and Nicole.

My thoughts turned to things that had happened in the not too distant past—things that troubled me about the relationship between Nicole and Bryant;

things I'd reluctantly dismissed, saying nothing about them to either of the girls. Bryant and Nicole were now arguing a lot. Bryant had begun calling me just wanting to talk. That was okay until he started telling me things I knew were not true. He suspected Nicole was cheating on him.

One night, Bryant said, he'd stopped by Nicole's apartment unexpectedly on his way home from his office. When he walked in quietly, she was stretched out on the sofa, caught up in her phone conversation. When Nicole saw him standing there, she was startled and abruptly ended her phone call. Well, I knew that was far from the truth because that was the night Nicole was at my place when Bryant and I were talking on the phone. Huh, but I never told Nicole.

Then there was the night he came over unexpectedly and just wanted to talk, again. He knew Tim had gone home to Iowa to visit his parents, but it was okay—innocent, nothing to it. After all, Bryant was Tim's friend and my girlfriend's fiancé. We did talk, he more than I, about the ghosts that were plaguing him.

When he finally decided it was time for him to leave, I felt a bit relieved and hoped that I had to helped him to dispel what I believed were surely myths in his head.

As I paused to say 'goodnight' at the door, my hand on the cold knob, Bryant grabbed my face and lifted it toward his as he swiftly and simultaneously brought his lips to mine in a bruising kiss. I quickly pushed him away, pain and anger evident on his face.

I was shocked and hurt. Not just hurt for myself but for my friend, Nicole, as well.

Then he started yelling about how Tim always got the best of everything, even the best woman! He stormed out the door slamming it behind him. I locked the door and stood there dazed. What had I done? How did this happen? When did this happen?

In a ball of confusion, I cried myself to sleep that night thinking of Bryant's sudden and apparent bitterness. Tim returned late that same night and came directly to my place before going to his apartment.

I said nothing to him about the incident with Bryant. I was just glad to have him home and to be back in his loving arms. Even when Tim said he knew I was okay while he was away because Bryant had promised d to come over and check on me, I still said nothing about it.

As I reflected on the past events, I could not help wondering if Nicole's marrying Bryant—at least right now—would be a mistake.

The following day Nicole, BettyMichelle and I met for lunch at Bratley's Café so we could discuss last minute preparations for our big wedding that was now just a couple of months away. Bratley's had been our favorite place for lunch ever since our freshman year at Bell. Before she could even speak, I noticed that Nicole seemed to be enveloped in sadness. As Betty Michelle and I chattered on and on about the final details and giggled with excitement, Nicole was quiet and distant.

Finally, after we'd shared a serving of our favorite chocolate pecan cheesecake, the dam broke. Through tears, Nicole explained that Bryant had been acting differently toward her. He'd even told her he felt like he was in love with someone else.

Now that would have been enough for me to call off wedding plans right then! But, she said, he'd countered that he was just going through pre-wedding jitters so they'd kissed and made up.

They what? BettyMichelle and I could only hope Nicole didn't see the look of shock, disbelief, and uncertainty on our faces.

The fall months were filled with so much to do; however, we went about our lives as normally as we could with ever present dreams of our fast approaching day. As teachers, we still had to be directors of learning no matter what was going on in our personal lives, so we worked in our classrooms with smiles on our faces.

We used most of the final days before our wedding consulting with our minister, Reverend Malloy. She was so excited for us all! The wedding director just happened to be Reverend Malloy's sister, Vinnie Malloy.

Wow! Our blessed day finally came. Everything went as planned and was absolutely beautiful! On New Year's Eve, 1979, we all seemed so much in love, even Bryant and Nicole. Our honeymoons carried us in different directions. Tim and I cruised to the Caribbeans; BettyMichelle and Gavin drove to the lovely, historic city of Charleston, South Carolina; and Nicole and Bryant flew to Las Vegas, Nevada, where they actually got tickets to see the famous "RatPack"—Frank Sinatra, Dean Martin, and Sammy Davis, Jr.

When we returned, we settled into married life and the next few years flew by as we lived our own private lives. But when friends don't keep in touch by calling or visiting often, something starts to happen. That something happened to us. The six friends, now three couples, began to drift apart. We each got caught up in our own little family world. I started taking graduate courses, and Tim became really involved coaching a third sport. Then we decided to have kids. Two came along making our family complete: and what had been busy, became busier.

Occasionally, we got together with the other two couples on holidays; then there would be long stretches where we wouldn't see each other at all. As years passed, we just seemed to spend less and less time together. Even the phone calls became fewer and less frequent.

BettyMichelle and Gavin, still living in Southport, had twin girls to keep them busy. Tim and I now had our two sons, Timothy, Jr. and Josh, and had moved to the town of Faith, six miles south of the city of Salisbury and about 290 miles from Southport. Nicole and Bryant, still together but childless, had moved to Baltimore, Maryland to be near Nicole's terminally ill mother who had been sadly diagnosed with lung cancer.

My phone conversations with Nicole were even fewer than those with BettyMichelle, and when I did talk with her she seemed a little distant—and with good reason, I guess, considering what she'd shared with me in a previous conversation. It went back to our freshman year at Bell, the day we missed the ferry and met the guys who eventually became our husbands. Bryant, she said, had once told her that he'd really wanted to talk to me that day, but Tim had gotten to me first. Surprised, I replied that I'd never known that. She laughed and commented about how silly and young we were then.

Our 10th year anniversary was approaching, and I had this wonderful idea that we should get together and have a grand celebration—an opportunity to renew our friendship, talk about old times, and catch up on what was going on in our lives. I called the others, and everyone agreed it was a great idea.

Right away I set about making the arrangements.

The plan was for us to meet at Grand Marcus Cabin Inn, an exclusive little winter resort nestled in the mountain town of Asheville, North Carolina. It would be perfect! It might even snow! Then we could really have a great time snowed in with best friends. Tim and I decided to visit the place beforehand to get a look at it.

By the next weekend, the sitter was at our house to keep our two boys, and Tim and I were off to the North Carolina Mountains. Grand Marcus Cabin Inn was everything the advertisements touted it to be and more: a majestic, serene, mountain setting. To stand on this spot and behold the beauty of nature was almost more than we could fathom. Tim and I seemed to fall in love all over again. We knew beyond a shadow of a doubt this was just the place for our planned reunion of friends.

That night was like a second honeymoon. With our favorite jazz playing softly, we ate a quiet supper by candle light. It was so different from the everyday suppers that had become a way of life with our boys— suppers where conversation was largely about their day, their friends, their interests and concerns.

That night, Tim and I engaged in some bona fide adult conversation and savored the taste of our food as well as our closeness to each other. We smiled, and "remembered when," and talked about the fun we would have when the Bell bunch gathered here in a few months.

When supper was finished, we tidied the kitchen. Then, grabbing our half-filled wine glasses, we settled onto the sofa where we cuddled under a blanket and watched a movie. The log in the fireplace had been reduced to a few glowing embers by the time we headed for our bedroom. We crawled into bed and into each other's arms. Oh, my Tim: my man, my love, my life! I wanted this moment etched in my mind for eternity.

The next night, the tranquility of our stay was shattered by the raucous behavior of some teenagers who Mr. Bert, the manager, later explained, had started to come to the resort on Saturday nights. He said they would sometimes get rowdy, drink liquor and beer, and once had actually gotten into a fist-fight with each other! Mr. Bert said the one who'd reserved their cabin had paid up front for every weekend of the winter months. Mr. Bert seemed more concerned that he'd gotten their money than he was concerned for the safety and comfort of the other guests.

The Berrys, an older couple we had met earlier in the day, explained how the hoodlums almost knocked them over on the sidewalk the night before and seemed not to care at all if they were hurt. "They laughed and kept on running," said Mrs. Berry disgustedly.

Mrs. Berry said she knew one of the boys and said he'd actually been arrested once for murder. "Somehow, though, he wormed his way out of the situation and was let go," she added.

It was our final night at the resort. The boys were playing their music way too loud, and the profanity was unbearable so Tim went over and asked them to please quiet down. They did—for about an hour; then the noise started again. I don't know how we finally got to sleep: just so exhausted I guess.

Wanting to make an early departure, we awakened the next morning just as the sun was rising. We had showered and dressed and were looking about to be sure we had packed everything when Tim and I noticed the boys from last night standing at our car. "What do you suppose they're up to?" I asked.

"I don't know," Tim replied, "but I'll see what I can find out."

With that, he grabbed one of our bags and walked out the door toward the car. I held my breath as I stood in the doorway.

"Excuse me," Tim said politely, but his politeness was

met with a hard shove. Reflexively, Tim dropped the bag and responded with a blow to his assailant's stomach. Just as quickly, I saw a glint of shiny metal in Tim's hand. I froze! Oh, no, I thought. But I knew Tim wouldn't use the knife except to scare them. Sensing their peril, the other teens grabbed their fallen friend and moved quickly toward their van. The one who Tim had pummeled, however, had one final warning for him: If he ever saw Tim again, he said, he would kill him!

On our way out, we reported the incident to Mr. Bert. He promised he would give the teens their money back and send them on their way with a warning. He said we shouldn't worry; the boys wouldn't be back. We took Mr. Bert at his word and spoke little of the incident or the teens themselves during our trip home. Frankly, I hardly even thought about it in the days and weeks that followed. I was more concerned about getting my friends on the phone to tell them more about the plans spinning in my head.

Of course, our boys were so excited to see us. They asked few questions about our trip; they were more interested in telling about their weekend. I waited until they were in bed for the evening before *three-waying* BettyMichelle and Nicole who wanted to know all about the place where we would be reuniting. I told them everything but didn't even think to mention the teens. Well, they wouldn't be there anyway—at least that's what Mr. Bert promised.

That call was the first of many planning sessions: what we were packing to wear, what CDs to bring, what food supplies, and especially the details of bringing in the New Year. We were bursting with excitement and anticipation. We could hardly wait to see each other! It would be just like old times.

Finally it was Christmas and then New Year's Eve. As Tim and I were driving up the interstate it began to snow. Oh, how beautiful! I loved snow and I felt it was following me to the cabin, falling just for all of us. I called to check on the kids. Mom had come over to spend the weekend with them at our house. Then Tim's parents flew in from Iowa. All four would still be there when we returned. Fortunately, our parents got along especially well with each other and they themselves were having a great time—with their grandsons and with each other. Everything seemed so perfect.

By the time we arrived at the Grand Marcus, the ground had welcomed an inch of new fallen snow. We succeeded in getting there early and getting our three-bedroom cabin in order before the others arrived. We got a warm fire going in the fireplace, stocked the wine bar, prepared a snack, started dinner, and set up the mini-stereo. About an hour later we heard laughter and talking just outside our cabin and immediately recognized the voices of BettyMichelle and Gavin. They were a lovely couple, still as much in love as Tim and I.

Before long, BettyMichelle and I were in the kitchen adding the finishing touches to dinner. The snacks were good, but nobody wanted to fill up on them. We'd save what was left of them for later that night or another day.

We all had driven quite a distance and our progress was slowed by the falling snow, so we were ready for a good hot meal. While BettyMichelle made the salad and set the table, I dealt with the rest of the meal including the casserole that was about ready to be taken from the oven.

All the while, we chattered like school girls. The guys had grabbed a couple of beers and were huddled in front of the TV cheering on one of their favorite teams. Like clockwork, Nicole and Bryant arrived just as I was taking the casserole out of the oven and popping in the rolls, but they brought with them a chill almost as cold as the mountain air. They seemed very distant and their conversation was strained; but, thank goodness, it wasn't long before they warmed up, and the wooden cabin was filled with love, laughter and conversation. It was just the way things had been when we were at Bell and during the year following our graduation.

After dinner, we loaded the dishes into the dishwasher and tidied the kitchen. Then we all retreated to the great room where we sipped wine, reminisced and listened to "old school" music: you know, the Dramatics and the Stylistics. At some point I went into the kitchen to get a tray of my dark chocolate brownies and was startled when Bryant suddenly appeared behind me. Standing almost too close for comfort, Bryant whispered into my ear how good I still looked and that I didn't need Tim, but needed him. I couldn't believe how crazy he could still be!

I let that go and quickly rejoined the rest of the group where the laughing, joking and remembrances continued. What a wonderful day it had been, everything we'd ever hoped for in this reunion! However, our long day coupled with the wine we'd consumed began to take its toll. It was past eleven o'clock. Determined to bring in the New Year together, we decided to prepare for bed but rejoin each other in the great room minutes before the stroke of midnight to sing *Auld Lang Syne* and make our New Year's toasts.

We were just about to head for our rooms when the loud music and profanity penetrated the night. Tim and I stared at each other in disbelief as the other couples questioned, "What in the world!" It can't be them, I thought. Tim and I didn't dare say we knew. We didn't want our friends to know about our previous encounter with the teens.

Tim called the main desk, but there was no answer. With a look of frustration, he turned to me and said, "I'm determined this is going to be a great weekend. I'm going over and put a stop to this once and for all." Bryant and Gavin quickly grabbed their jackets insisting on going with him.

As they headed out the door, I heard Tim begin to tell them about our encounter with the teens.

The guys stayed and stayed; Nicole, BettyMichelle and I grew weary waiting. It certainly was taking them an awfully long time.

It was now five minutes before midnight and we wanted to ring in the New Year, 1989, together, just like we had done ten years ago. Finally, as the clock struck midnight, Gavin rushed into the great room. He grabbed the phone and dialed a few numbers speaking excitedly..

"Everything happened so fast," he was saying and we quickly realized he was talking to the 911 dispatcher, confirming that the two squad cars dispatched to the area had arrived. That's when I noticed the bright blue lights of the police cars. We three reacted at once, bombarding Gavin with a cacophony of questions.

Suddenly a hush blanketed the room as we saw the police with Bryant in handcuffs. I looked for my Tim, but all I could see was a covered body being taken away on a stretcher. I heard the teens talking and one of them was crying to Mr. Bert. Then Gavin recounted the horrible series of events.

Tim, Gavin and Bryant had first gone to the office to report the disturbance, but they found no one there. Maybe it was because it was a holiday; maybe because it was almost midnight. Now even more annoyed, they headed for the cabin from which the loud music blared and pounded on the door several times before one of the boys flung it open spewing profanities. Gavin said Tim had fussed the boys out and the teens had jumped to fight, but eventually Tim was able to bring them under control without anyone getting physical, until one of the teens asked wasn't he the same old dude from a couple of months ago.

When Tim answered 'yes', Gavin said, to his surprise, the kid politely replied, "I'm so sorry about that." The boy also said they had promised Mr. Bert they would be good so he would allow them to come back on weekends. He added that they hadn't realized how loud the music was. As the young fellow went to lower the volume on their stereo, Tim softly boasted jokingly, "Yeah, I thought you'd better do that."

Suddenly Bryant, not one of the teens, shouted at Tim using profanity, telling Tim how he must think he's so cool and so important!

He accused Tim of always thinking himself the best and how much he hated Tim: that he hated Tim for taking the one and only woman he had ever loved, how he had fallen in love with me first, and how Tim thought he was always supposed to get the best of everything!

He went into a total rage pulling out a gun and shooting Tim in the head! My Tim—the love of my life, my children's father, the man God gave to me—was no longer with us! Tim was dead!

We buried the husband, the father, the son, the friend we all loved in his hometown of Burl, Iowa on a cold, snowy January afternoon while Bryant settled in for a long prison stay. Gavin, BettyMichelle, and even Nicole were by my side.

We still keep in touch, the three of us girls. Well, really the six of us. I am now remarried to Gavin's brother, Bill. He is a wonderful man and a sincere father to my Josh and Timothy, Jr. We met at the funeral and started dating two years later. The third year, we were married. It was a double ceremony this time. You see, Nicole married Bill's twin, Will, and we all are living happily ever after.

FAMILY INEVITABILITY

THE LETTERS—Part I
A LETTER TO CAROL

Dear Carol,

It's been a long day, but I will not let it end without thanking you. See, you don't really know me or maybe wouldn't even recognize me, but I just met you again since ….

Well, do you recall this morning when you were on Highway 55 driving toward Lancaster? I'm sure you do. I see you every morning. Yea, you drive that '09 Mazda. The green one with the gold trim; clean tires, too, I must say. Then the plate on the front: *Carol Ann Beshaw*. Every morning around 7:30, I wait.

When you get to the Break-fast Bar on Park and Fulton I watch you get out, go inside and then return with a cup. The aromas from the restaurant fill my nostrils as I watch and wait.

I've never gotten the nerve to approach you. You've never even looked my way, but I must say you always look lovely: dressed so chic and stepping with so much confidence. I like that in a woman.

This morning was a little different though. Things were a little bit out of balance and you dropped your bag. You never noticed your little purse had fallen out of your pocketbook. You quickly jumped into your Mazda and sped off. I ran over and grabbed it before anyone else could. Inside was a comb, lip gloss, a small red mirror, a pastel purple colored ink pen, a clean folded sheet of paper, a book of stamps, pieces of a torn picture of a man (your fellow maybe?) and *bingo*: your ID card—oh yea, and a folded hundred dollar bill.

The money would have been a blessing to someone else like me, but your identity was all that I was interested in. Now I know for sure you are Carol Ann Beshaw: the same Carol Ann Beshaw who sat beside me in Business 101 back in '76 at Jordan College in Lancaster; the same girl who would let me copy her homework. That's the only reason I recalled the name on your car.

In Business 101 you did everything you could to get my attention, and I knew what you were doing. But me—"*the man*", the coolest dude at Jordan, the fraternity jock—looking even once at a fat, short-haired girl like you? Oh no! I could get any girl I wanted; and believe me, I got everyone I wanted, too. Though, the last one, dug in deep and got me.

I also remember how you would always stare at me. To this day your eyes remind me of someone else's. It was almost scary. Then there were times when I was almost in a fight, and you would run to see if I were okay. I would always tell you to get out of my face and leave me alone.

You see Carol, after I graduated from Jordan, I didn't stop there. I went on to Billings School of Law and later joined my father's law firm: Parker, Brown and Blount. His partner, the mighty Attorney John Seymour Blount, had already chosen me to be his son-in-law. To make a long story short: my parents—well, my dad—told me I had to marry Blount's daughter "to keep it all in the business." My mother never really approved of her. She said the girl was not honest and a marriage without love and honesty wouldn't last. But you know: it was all good.

We had everything we wanted, the money, a mansion of a home, big cars, the works; and she was super fine. In fact, she was too fine: so fine that one night I went back to the office and caught her with my father. Yep! Caught them in an intimate way. I knew she was seeing somebody, but never would I have thought it was he! That short, old, ….

I noticed he never dated anyone after my mother died. She died a month after I got married to that witch. I loved my mother whose face, I'm proud to say, I can still see each time I look in a mirror. I am her only child, and our resemblance is striking. It was my wife's idea to have dad move in with us "because he will be lonesome," she begged so pitifully. She also convinced my father and me to put the money he gained from selling his home into a fund for our future children. She told us she would go to the bank and take care of everything "since we were so busy."

However, the banker told her she would have to come back with my father to do that type of transaction. I later learned from the banker that she'd told him she was my father's daughter, Carol B. Parker. Well, her name was Carol Parker, but she'd only gotten the name Parker by marrying me. Of course I didn't go with her to the bank. Can you believe I trusted her at one time? I also found out that she didn't want my father or me to go to the bank because she didn't deposit all of the money. She kept a sizeable sum for herself.

The little hussy got really angry when the banker told her she couldn't touch the money until our future child was 18 years old. When she didn't want to start a family, Carol began spending more lavishly. She started going away on weekends. I knew our relationship would not last. In retrospect, her weekends away were always the same weekends my father was away at golf tournaments.

Getting back to the dreadful night that changed my life. When I walked into the office, the two of them were so involved they didn't even notice I was there. I pulled my pistol from my drop leg holster. I had made a habit of always carrying it at night. I pointed it at them as she glanced my way and pushed my father off of her. He fell against me and the pistol discharged. He died instantly. I did my time as a murderer, but the good behavior act was on my side. I got out of Bently State Pen in April. She went free, not even a question asked.

For the last three months, I've been living on the streets, begging. I saw her one time riding with Phil

Brown, the son of my father's other partner. I heard another homeless dude say, "That couple lives out at the Parker mansion."

The Parker mansion? No freaking way! That used to be our home.

Now, I have nothing left but the clothes on my back, an old knapsack, my spot against the wall of the underpass near the Break-Fast Bar, and three other homeless friends: three talented, former restoration workers who are out of work and down on their luck.

Thomkins, the manager at the Break-Fast Bar, gave me your address. I listed each item in the paragraph above so you will know that I am honest. I am returning all of your belongings, except two things. I used the folded piece of paper and the pastel purple colored ink pen to write this letter and four of your stamps to mail the package. I hope you don't mind. Thomkins promised to mail it with his business mail tomorrow.

Maybe I shouldn't have written so much. I really don't mean to bore you. I hope you will find it in your heart to somehow forgive me for the way I treated you back in college. I'm a changed man. It seems that while I was in prison I had a lot of time to think. You were often in my thoughts. I received anonymous letters and packages and finally figured out the sender must have been my mother's cousin, Ree. She lived near Bently State. I never had visitors except the minister who told me about Jesus and that my soul being saved was much more important than anything else. That is why I have to do the right thing and send back your belongings—the folded one hundred dollar bill, too—and most of all, to say I'm sorry.

Your college acquaintance,

Jerald Dallas Parker

THE LETTERS—Part 2
RESPONSE TO JERALD

Dear Jerald,

I know Mr. Thomkins because I stop to buy coffee at his restaurant every morning. Next time I see him, I will thank him for mailing the package. However, the biggest thanks goes to you. I was going crazy looking everywhere for my purse. I didn't realize I had dropped it on the street in front of the restaurant. Thank you a million times!

Yes, yes, yes: I remember you! I will never forget you! I am sorry you had to go through such tragedies in your life. Actually, I know a little bit more about the incident you mentioned and far more about you and your life than you'd ever imagine!

First and foremost, let me say that I forgive you. I forgave you a long time ago.

You see, Jerald, my life has been pretty splendid. From the first day I saw you and learned your name, I knew I had to be there for you: to make sure you passed tests, to help heal your wounds, to make sure you were alright. Now, I apologize for not making it known that it was I who sent those things to you in prison.

When I heard about the tragic death of your father, your mother's dying, and of you going to prison, I knew you would need someone. I wasn't sure how you would respond to me as a visitor, so I kept everything anonymous.

No one would tell me where you went when you left prison, so I must say I was happier to actually hear from you than I was about getting my purse back.

As I said before, my life has been splendid. Perhaps you have heard of the *Beshaw Computer Sales and Service* chain that has expanded to two states. I am the proud owner of that chain. I have twelve stores in this state and ten in Georgia. I'm working toward opening two stores in Virginia this year. My office headquarters is, of course, here in Lancaster.

I've chosen to stay here because Mother lives with me; she would never get used to living any place else. She's in excellent health for her seventy-six years. We have a relatively modest home in a cul-de-sac on the lake off Crescent. I hope you like that area because I am inviting you to come visit. No, not come visit, but come stay. The reason for this invitation isn't just that I'm a good, sweet, Christian girl; rather, it's for a reason of which you haven't a clue.

Through the years, I asked my mother time and again to tell me who my daddy was, but she always brushed me off, saying, "You are fine without him, so stop asking me."

One night I heard my mother crying softly in her bedroom and went to see what was wrong. I gathered her into my arms, softly stroking her back and arms and whispering reassurances, hoping she would open up to me. Finally, she explained how she really wanted me to attend college, but knew she didn't have the money. I told her I didn't have to go to college, that I would just stay at home and get a job at the mill.

My mother didn't want to hear that. She knew I had

always dreamed of going to college even as a very young child, and she wanted that dream to come true. I boldly told her that it was time for my daddy, whoever he was, to step in and help. I begged her to please tell me who he was, but as in the past, her lips were sealed.

Time passed, and the summer before I entered Jordan College, Mama came home one afternoon after working all day in that hot florist. She told me she had spoken with my father. She said that he'd promised to help me with college. In exchange, however, she had to promise she would never reveal his name.

I insisted it was not fair to me that I didn't know his identity. My mother looked at me with tears in her eyes and told me she was too ashamed to tell because she was not in love with him nor was he in love with her when I was conceived. My sweet mother told me that my existence was the result of rape, committed by a well known public figure in the local community.

Your father, Jerald, raped my mother. You and I share the same blood.

Mother made me promise to never try to find him or ever breathe this secret to anyone. She said no one would have believed her if she'd told the story then, and no one would believe her now.

That, Jerald, is why I had to look out for you. You are my brother.

My mother always said I had "his eyes," but she thanked God because I resembled her more. The torn picture is one I cut from an advertisement in the *Lancaster Herald* many years ago.

I was pondering the whole scene yesterday as I was driving to work and became so upset that I tore the picture up and dropped the pieces into the purse that you found.

I was upset because my mother had another really bad nightmare a couple of nights ago: a recurring nightmare that has haunted her for many years. She dreams that he is coming after her to do her harm.

Yes, the chubby, short-haired girl you tried to avoid in college is me: Carol Ann Beshaw, your sister.

More surprises!

This morning I got a call from a lawyer who wants to meet with Mom and me to go over the contents of a recently found folder tucked inside an old metal box with our names engraved on it and hidden in the boards of the Parker mansion.

I hate to tell you, but the mansion burned a few weeks ago.

After sifting through the ashes, the only thing recovered was the metal box that had a few smudges, but the contents were in perfect shape.

For once in his life, your daddy—our daddy—must have felt guilty. Among other things, the contents contained a will stipulating that everything he owned was to be given to his daughter at his passing. I am his only daughter!

What a tragedy. Your beautiful ex-wife wasn't as smart as she thought. Just as you said, she put the "fund" money in the Parker account under the name Carol and told the banker she was your father's daughter.

Yep, I now know her name is Carol also, but I am the only daughter your father had. The lawyer that called me explained that all of the money and interest gained belong to me, and what's left of Parker house belongs to you, Jerald. Your ex-wife has nothing.

No, Carol B. Parker didn't perish in the fire. She wasn't even at home. According to the *Lancaster Herald*, her husband, Phil Brown, was in jail all night after being arrested for threatening to kill her when he caught her at the Night Light Hotel. Her car was still parked there when I passed the hotel the next morning, and so was the car belonging to our father's other partner, Jake Blount. Coincidence?

Now, before we start to contemplate restoring the burned mansion, I want you to be ready when I come to pick you up in my '09 Mazda with the gold trim and clean tires. I will meet you for lunch at the Break-fast Bar tomorrow. I think you know where that is. Spend one more day with your friends. May I suggest: If they pitch in and help restore it, they could use the mansion as their new home, but you are coming home to live with me and a mom that's as sweet as yours was.

Sincerely,

Your sister, Carol

.

LOVE AND HAPPINESS

WITHOUT YOU I CAN'T BREATHE

Love is a sample of heaven:
Mate, children and grandchildren –
chosen by God.
Depending on your hearts to beat
Is to live,
To exist,
To matter in this world.
Our love didn't just happen –
It was all part of God's plan.
You all are my life –
The reason I wake each morning.
Without you,
I can't breathe.

PREVAILING CONDITIONS

CONTENTMENT

Morning demitasse, cream but no froth
On a breezy winter day.

Raindrops ping-panging my roof
With no particular place to go.

A whistling young lad
With wiggling toes out of socks.

The deft of the piano jazz next door—
Music that just had to float
Through my open window.

A frivolous joke
Told by my adult daughter.

Sparks of love when eyes meet—
My husband, his wife, us
Even after thirty-something.

Night sounds send satisfied messages:
Soft snores, frogs croaking for moisture,
A clock tick-tocking

It's my house.
I love living here.
I'm pleased.

I need no new frontier.
Peace of mind is my best friend.
Contentment.

UNNATURAL

'CAUSE GRANNY DON'T LIE

It was back, way back, when times were real. It was when winter was cold with snowdrifts, and icicles formed a tasty treat when broken from the tip of old tin roofs. It was when spring came with flowers, and Easter morning was breakfast time with fish, grits, and deviled eggs.

It was a time, a real time, when leaves fell in the fall, and you could smell the smoke of their cremation as your head turned to the melodies of the local fair merrymaking: as your nostrils welcomed the smell of grilled onions, and your mouth watered to be covered with candy apple red. It was back, way back, when summer was really hot: so hot watermelon juice dripped and mingled with sweat, and ice cream melted through your fingers.

It was then that she was in her prime. She could see, touch, taste, feel, and hear things that no one else could. She could make dreams come true for my future: a future she didn't even know—neither did I know.

It has become my healing, her love. Writing about her gives me peace of mind. Her stories tell time. She, my Granny Rose, had always been there. I'd often thought, maybe she had already been to heaven and was sent back to watch over us. I don't think she was real; just an angelic spirit in flesh. She went back just when she and her best friend, God, got ready; but before she left, she told me stories.

I remember that time Granny Rose told me and my brothers and sisters this one. It was a summer day back in '67. Now if you got a weak heart or just plain can't stand scary stuff, stop reading now! Put this away! I've warned you! 'Cause see, it's messed up and 'cause Granny don't lie.

It happened as such, me and my big sista Barbra had to go down to the old creek in the Gulf. Now that's a little town in Chatham County, N.C. The Gulf is where I was raised. I was born over near Taylor's Chapel. You young'uns didn't know about that, did ya?

"Naw!" we blurted, our eyes stretched wide because Granny already had our attention.

Oh, there's plenty of hants in Gulf, even now! Humph! I don't want to scare you young'uns, but when me and my sista went down that long path through them woods back of Aunt Bea's, we saw a hant that day.

"What's a hant?" I asked.

Hush child! A hant's like a ghost.

Well anyhow, we had to wash clothes at Frazier Creek. That was back in 1917 or '18. We didn't know nothin' about washin' machines and 'lectric stuff. We couldn't even afford one of them new washboards. The boil pot was kept down by the bank full of water from the creek. We built a little fire around that pot to get the water real hot. We would wash the white clothes first, with lye soap, then the colored clothes. I had my piece of lye ready when I heard the bushes cracking and saw 'em moving.

"What's that?" Barbra asked me real scared like as she

stopped dead still in the middle of what she was doing. Told her I didn't know: some little varmint, I reckon. Lawd chillun, when I turned around, I saw this little old dwarf.

"Did he look like Uncle Umps?" my brother, Lynn, interrupted curiously.

Naw, you know your uncle is just a midget, not a dwarf, and hush! I can't even tell the story for y'all keep buttin' in. I got to hurry up. I got to start making them biscuits 'fore supper and 'fore your uncle gets back with that 'lasses."

Well, anyhow, I said to that little old man: "Hey, what you doing here on our papa's land?"

He was standing real still and had on some old, dirty tore up clothes. He had pointed ears and his skin was the color of ash. He never spoke a word, just held up a cane with a carved wolf's head for the handle.

It scared me and Barbra so bad 'cause the wolf had yellow teeth and red glowing eyes.

Me and Barbra started screaming and chunking rocks at him. I don't know if I fainted or what, but when I got back in this world, he had vanished.

Lawd chillun, my sista and me stomped out that fire, grabbed up some of them clothes, and hightailed it back to the house! We fell up on that old plank porch. Mama heard us and came rushing out, the screen door banging shut behind her.

"What's wrong with y'all?" she huffed. "You gonna wake up Baby Lizzie!"

Papa was coming up from the cow pasture. "You chilluns look like you done saw a hant or sump'n," he laughed.

We got in that house, and me and Barbra started talking at the same time.

"Who was that little man, Granny Rose?" my sister Angela asked.

I hate to tell you chilluns anything. You don't listen long enough 'fore you start wanting to know sump'n else! Hush! Let me finish!

Well, when me and Barbra started tellin' Mama and Papa about that doggone little dwarf man, the part I'll never forget is 'bout my mama, what she did. That big proud woman that kept us from all danger and harm fell on her knees and started praying to the Almighty, justa praying to beat the band! She was speaking to Him so fast…"

"Well, was she speaking in tongues?" my brother, Des, inquired, scared to death.

Hush! Shh! Don't you talk about tongues! That's grown-folks' church talk.

Well anyhow, Mama was scared to death. Then what Papa did made me almost die a big fat death right then! "Lawd Maude, what we gonna do?" he pleaded to my mama for a answer.

He ran out to the end of the road and started ringing that old rusty bell hooked onto the rotted part of that raggedy fence with the peeling white paint. I'd done seen that old bell posted there all my life, but I never knew why it was there.

For the first time, I thought 'bout sump'n': Everybody in the Gulf had a old rusty bell on they fence or porch or somewhere in the yard.

In a flash you could hear the sound of another bell, then another, and then more as the sounds faded into the distance. Dogs started howling and the sky turned gray as I watched my papa sweating and shaking with fear. I knew the other bell sounds came from our neighbors who lived on down the old ten mile dirt road. Mama grabbed some biscuits and fatback off the now cold wood cooking stove in the kitchen. She put the food in our hands and pushed us back into the bedroom we all three shared.

"This is for y'all to eat on today and tonight," Mama said with tears and fright in her eyes.

By then Papa had done come back in. I peeped out of the curtain that posed as our privacy door. I saw him nailing up boards to the windows, the doors, the cracks—everywhere and anywhere a creature big or small, animal or human, or even a hant might could get in.

It's one thing to see your mama scared, but Lawd knows when I saw my big strong 300 pound papa's nose twitching, lips moving with no sound, and his whole body shaking like a leaf on a tree over this little dwarf man, I was a goner. He stopped long enough to get the Bible off the wood chest and threw it to Mama, and he ordered her to "Start reading, gal!"

"'Yea, though I walk through the valley and the shadow of death, I will fear no evil: for thou art with me; thy rod and thy staff they comfort me.'"

I believe this was around Easter in 1918. I do remember it was late spring and with everything boarded up, it was hot up in that old house! Now, the really scary part happened later that night. I was gonna be brave, so I called out, "Mama, who is that man? Why y'all scared of him?"

"Just be quiet!" she hissed through her teeth.

Little Lizzy woke up, and I fed her some of my biscuit and meat. Barbra woke up then, and we took turns rocking our baby sista back to sleep while we talked below a whisper and a notch above lip-reading. Mama and Papa came in, checked on us, gave us water and some more biscuits.

By then it was night time. Lizzie fell back to sleep. I put her in her little cradle that Papa had first made for my big sista Barbra, and they say I used to sleep in it, too.

The last time Mama came in, she told us to get in the bed. Me and Barbra shared a bed. She always slept on the backside facing the wall, and I slept on the front. We did what Mama told us to do. In a little while, I could hear Barbra and Lizzie snoring. I was too hot to sleep. I could hear Mama and Papa whispering. Finally, I must have fallen off to sleep, but let me tell you sump'n'.

Over in the night, I woke up. It was so miser'bly hot, I couldn't sleep for long. As my eyes peeled opened, I looked right eye level into the eyes of that little dwarf man! I still feel goose bumps rising as I remember those red eyes.

I don't know if I passed out or what or if his magic put me back to sleep, but when I woke the next morning, I was on the back side of the bed and Barbra was on the front! My blood-curdlin' scream, louder than a morning rooster, woke up ever'body.

Barbra asked, "How'd I get over here and you over yonder?"

"I don't know," I told her as Mama and Papa rushed in and Lizzie started to cry, "but I know one thing for sure. He came in here last night! He came to me! Who is he, Papa? Tell me, please! I'm scared!"

With sweat still pouring, Papa started to explain the unknown: "It's him, 'the evil one.' He come back ever' now and then to gather some of his kind. Watch what I tell you.

"Some of them ole mean folks 'round here, you won't

see 'em no more. Bob Sealy who killed that little girl down by the river claimin' it was a accident, Bo Tomkins who shot his wife so he could have another wife, Tom Jells who beats his chilluns for no reason, ….you'll never see any of 'em again.

"And you know what chilluns? We hadn't heard hair nor tail of him, the one they call 'the evil one,' since I was a child in my teens. You 'member, don't you, Maude? We was both goin' to the old one room school then. Hadn't heard hair nor tail of him no more. That is, not 'til yesterday when y'all seen him down there at Frazier Creek," Papa said with the sound of trepidation still in his voice.

"Honey, don't you gals worry," was all Mama could say. "He didn't get in here. Must've been a bad dream you had, Rose."

I looked at my loving mama real long and hard. Then I asked slowly, "Well, if he didn't come in, then where did that wolf-head cane over yonder come from?"

❧

As Granny Rose got up and started to make her biscuits, she told us all to go on and do our chores.

 "Granny, what happened to that cane? The wolf-head

cane, with the red eyes and the yellow teeth?"

"Now, Honey, that's for me to know, and you don't want to find out," was all my Granny Rose would say. "But what I told y'all is the truth, 'cause Granny don't lie."

UNCOMMON FAVOR

SACRED TALE

Well, let me think back on how and when I met Sissy.
I was walking along the wooded trail back of our old
farmhouse minding my own when I heard a slight
moan. It was a warm breezy Saturday morning in
Glendale, a little town in central North Carolina.
Hmmm, Glendale: my little hometown where I was
born and had lived all my life.

Thinking back, I was minding my own, when the
second sound of moaning, slightly weaker, was heard.
So I called out, asking, "Who's that?" No answer, of
course. I tipped closer to the old abandoned barn and
that's when I saw her: a beautiful brown-skinned
young girl with reddish pigtails, covered with an old

piece of burlap and lying upon a mildly built bed of hay. I asked her what she was doing there and was she hurt. She was so frightened! She asked me to please leave her alone; said she was too weak to fight anymore. Now I wasn't a fighter; however, at that point I could have been labeled a fourteen year old scary cat.

Her face was flushed with grooves of cuts; and her pigtails, as they rested upon bruised shoulders, were matted with straw and pieces of leaves. I explained to her that I would never hurt anyone.

She tried to sit up a bit and that's when I noticed her belly was huge. She was with child. Too young to be that way, but she was.

I handed her my bottle of ice water that I just happened to put in my overalls pocket. She took a few swigs watching me carefully. She must have gained confidence in my character then 'cause she just turned the bottle up and didn't let it drop until all of the liquid was gone, completely.

Within the next hour I learned her name was Sisstine, but everybody called her Sissy. She was fifteen years old and had no siblings. Her dad, the love of her life, had died in the Vietnam War three years ago. She said that was when all of her troubles started.

Her mother, whom she always suspected was not being true to her father, remarried last year to a man she called Mr. Paul. Mmm-humph, the same Mr. Paul she had seen sneaking out of the back porch door some mornings while her dad was overseas fighting for our country; the same Mr. Paul who had actually invited her father on a weekend hunting trip once when he was home on leave.

On that particular run-of-the-mill outing, Mr. Paul "accidentally" shot her dad. However, her dad, Harold Lloyd Timpson, was a strong man, a soldier; and that bullet was just a scar to him after it was removed from his left shoulder. It was that same Mr. Paul who was by her mama's side at her daddy's funeral, and the same low down dog that raped her constantly for the last year: the same man who her mama believed when Sissy told her she was sick—that something was wrong.

Mr. Paul, you see, told Sissy's mama that he had seen a young fella named Lucus Smelt coming out of Sissy's bedroom window one night when Paul himself was coming in late. Of course that was a lie, but her mama believed it. Sissy said Mr. Paul told her to get out and go find somewhere to have that baby.

Sissy explained further that she packed as much food as she could, and got in the car with Mr. Paul just like Mr. Paul told her. Then he drove Sissy here to this place. He hadn't even allowed her to tell her mother good-bye. Sissy figured her mother would be glad she was out of the way. Her mother was always high on something and probably wouldn't miss her for a while anyway.

After they had been driving about two hours, Mr. Paul stopped the car on the main highway. He nodded for Sissy to open the door and looked at her as if she knew to get out of the car. Following his silent command, she slowly opened the door and just as slowly began to climb out, too slow for him.

He reached over and gave her a shove that toppled her onto the pavement and sent her tumbling down a slight hill.

She really didn't know where she was. She only knew where she was from: a place called Grove, South Carolina.

She had made it about a mile through the woods when she stumbled upon this old barn and had to rest. She was in terrible pain. I learned a lesson that day, quick. I grew up in one day! I told her to stay still; I would go and get help.

Sissy was so frightened she didn't want me to leave, but I turned and didn't look back. I ran all the way home and found just who I needed—Grandma Shirl!

I knew my grandma wouldn't let a good soul down and would be willing to help. I was even happier when I discovered she was the only one at home. My mom had gone to buy groceries in town. I explained to Grandma what I had encountered as I walked through the woods on my day off.

After telling me I had no business being out there, she got her walking stick and I led the way.

We heard her this time, louder, as we got nearer. When we reached that old barn, Sissy was breathing hard but hanging in there. We helped her sit up, and then got her to stand and walk a little by holding on to me and Grandma Shirl.

Grandma Shirl told Sissy we were going to get her to our house, but she was going to have to help us. I wasn't too sure walking her from that barn to our house was a good thing in her condition, but Grandma Shirl knew a lot more about such things, so I kept my mouth shut and just followed Grandma Shirl's lead.

It was a slow struggle, but we finally made it.

We lived in a two-story, weather-beaten farmhouse with four bedrooms. One of them was mine and one was Grandma Shirl's. One belonged to my mama, Peggy, and my dad; but he'd died from lung cancer in 1961 when I was 6 years old. The fourth bedroom was the guest bedroom and that's where we tried to make Sissy as comfortable as we could: you know, under the circumstances.

Grandma Shirl called her friend Sadie Jakes, a local midwife, and she came right away. By midnight on June 15, 1969, we finally had another boy in our house—Jason Marell Timpson.

It was a bit strange having a baby in the house. Mama and Grandma Shirl treated that baby like a prince. So did I. We all got used to each other: Sissy and me; Sissy and the ladies. All of us got used to the baby, and he got used to us.

When school opened in the fall, Sissy was on that bus with me. We told everyone she and the baby were our cousins from South Carolina. She fit right in with me and my friends. There was one thing different about Sissy, though: she was extremely smart! She was what the school folks today would call "academically gifted." She made super grades, helped at home and took care of her baby, and she never got behind in her classes. I must say, she also helped me get better grades, too. She was always telling me how her father said, "Getting an education is the most important thing to accomplish in life."

Now along with her school work, she enjoyed skating and bowling and going to the school ball games, but she was never interested in dating anyone. I think what happened to her with that stepfather was enough. Baby Jay grew healthy and happy. Grandma, Mama, and Sissy made sure of that.

Sissy and I both had jobs. I saved every penny I earned from working part-time at Mr. Blake's store, and Sissy did the same. She worked evenings five hours at Whirl Burger. We were both determined to enter a private college in Raleigh, North Carolina after graduation. Sissy graduated top in our high school class in 1973; and let's just say, I graduated, too.

We worked hard at the private college and our grades showed it. Sissy pledged Delta Sigma Theta and I pledged Omega Psi Phi. Mama, Grandma Shirl and eight year old Jay, of course, were proud to be on the front row to see us both get our Bachelor of Arts and Bachelor of Science degrees.

I got a job right away as a physical education teacher at Glendale Elementary. My girlfriend, Beverly, worked as a P.E. teacher as well, across town at the junior high. She was also a physical education major at the same college with Sissy and me.

Sissy was still working part-time in Raleigh and saving as much money as she could. In the fall, she entered Carolina Central in Durham. She didn't stop that education stuff until she'd become a lawyer in Raleigh and headed her own firm. She and her son lived a happy life and came to visit often. She never once mentioned her mother, Mr. Paul, or any of those bad times—and none of them ever came looking for her.

As the years passed, Beverly and I got married and moved into a nice apartment near downtown Glendale. I couldn't go too far from Mama, Grandma Shirl and, of course, my little buddy Jay who, by the time he was thirteen, was extremely talented in basketball. He was a starter on his junior high school's basketball team, and we never missed any of his games even if it meant we had to drive forty miles. Sometimes we even followed him out of state.

He became a top player in high school, and when it was time for him to choose a college, he had plenty to choose from. Not only was he a great player, but he was academically gifted like his mother. He chose St. Thomas, and how happy we were! Everyone thought he would choose an ACC school, but he wanted to follow in his mom's and my footsteps.

After school one day, when I was reading the local newspaper in the school library, I noticed an ad about finding ancestors or anyone you wanted to locate. A website was mentioned so, on a hunch, I went straight to a computer and keyed in the required information. Bingo! Up popped the name "Martha Timpson Stewart," Sissy's mother! She was listed as deceased. I navigated to the website of Grove, South Carolina's local newspaper.

Once there, I pulled up the obituaries section and clicked on the "Past Thirty Years" tab. There it was plain as day: the whole death announcement. There was even a picture of Martha Timpson Stewart and her daughters, Sisstine Timpson (whereabouts unknown) and the "late" Misstine Timpson. The two girls looked identical! It blew my mind. I couldn't stop there. I was driven!

I clicked back to the site's home page, went straight to the archives (May, 1979) and the local news. My heart began racing when I saw the headline, "Local Lumber Worker Kills Wife." As I read further, I almost passed out:

Local lumber worker, Paul Stewart, killed his beloved wife Martha Timpson Stewart .... Paul Stewart's body reeked of alcohol when local law enforcement officers rushed into his home at 495 Sycamore Street here in Grove last night. Neighbors called police to report screams and the sounds of glass and furniture breaking. They reported hearing a gunshot, then dead silence. When questioned about the incident, several neighbors said the sounds of fussing and fighting at this residence were commonplace.

Paul reportedly had harbored a growing anger since his wife had confessed to him she'd been having an affair with her daughter Sissy's friend, Lucus Smelt. When Smelt was questioned, he admitted he'd started seeing Mrs. Stewart right there in her home the year he turned seventeen. He would sneak in when Mr. Stewart was dead drunk. "Mrs. Stewart always paid me for my services," Lucus Smelt told investigating officers.

Like Paul Stewart, neighbors who were aware of Smelt's clandestine comings and goings, thought he was sneaking in to see Mrs. Stewart's daughter, Sisstine Timpson who ironically, head-lined local papers when she suddenly went missing in 1969. Smelt has always been a person of interest in the disappearance of Sisstine "Sissy" Timpson.

Smelt was later imprisoned for the attempted murder of Paul Stewart's brother, Bob Stewart. In an altercation at Blend's Bar, a local nightclub, Smelt shot Bob Stewart in the neck after an argument over a pool bet.

Smelt, who still lives in Grove, South Carolina, recalled having received a call from Martha Timpson Stewart no sooner than he was released from prison. Smelt said Mrs. Stewart told him in that call, it would be good to see him again, and she never believed he had anything to do with the sudden disappearance of her daughter. Smelt has always maintained his innocence and says he does not know what happened to Sissy Timpson.

Funeral arrangements for Mrs. Martha Timpson Stewart are incomplete.

Wow! So, Sissy had a twin sister! In all these years, why hadn't she ever mentioned her? Her mother is dead and her stepfather, in prison for murder. So, does Sissy think her twin sister, Missy, is missing or dead, or does she even know she had a twin sister? I had so many questions.

My drive home that afternoon seemed to take longer than ever. No sooner than Bev walked in the door, I hit her with the news that I had stumbled upon in the school library. I was babbling like a kid, so excited that she had to slow me down. Bev listened with as much amazement as I had when I was reading the article I'd found in the newspaper's archives. She agreed this news merited an immediate family get-together so I was on the phone right away.

I called Sissy and asked her to please come home to Mom and Grandma Shirl's tomorrow and to be prepared to spend the weekend. I called Jay, now in his senior year at St. Thomas, and told him to get his red Mustang on the road home for the weekend. Finally, I called Mom and told her we would all be home. She was overjoyed and immediately wanted to know what she needed to start cooking. She shouted the news to Grandma Shirl whose joyous yelps I could hear in the background. It was to be a weekend I would never forget.

After all the telephoning, Bev and I resumed our conversation. We had been in deep discussion for more than an hour when she suddenly asked, "What are we waiting for? Let's go to Grove and visit Mr. Smelt—if he's still around. Maybe he can help us with this puzzle."

She didn't have to say it twice.

Beverly and I were packed and on the road to Grove in record time. We arrived about ten o'clock that same night and checked into the Starr Hotel on Maple Street in the downtown area.

Once in our room, I dropped our bags on the floor and made for the telephone directory, searching for the name Lucus Smelt. I was surprised to find the number listed especially since he had spent time in prison, and I thought it nothing short of miraculous that he answered on the first ring at such a late hour. I guess when God is on your side, things just seem to fall in place; and I felt like I was on a divinely inspired mission.

I briefly introduced myself then told Mr. Smelt I had some interesting news about Sisstine Timpson that might change his life forever. Immediately he explained, quite nervously, that he had not had any contact with Sissy Timpson since she had returned to Grove. For a moment I was speechless and asked what he was talking about. Sissy wasn't back in Grove. "Oh yes, she is," Smelt insisted. "She's back, living in her family's old house on Sycamore Street."

"Then we really need to talk—immediately," I said.

Although it was late and he sounded unsure, Smelt agreed to come to the hotel lobby. I hung up and called the office of the local sheriff telling them the short version of my story and asking if someone from his office could meet us in the lobby. I don't think they believed me at first, but he and one of his men showed up anyway.

Smelt arrived first just as I had hoped he would. The sheriff's vehicle pulled up about twenty minutes later. With Bev by my side, I told the whole story. No one interrupted, but the men did ask several questions when I had finished. They seemed convinced but still shook their heads in disbelief.

It was now approaching midnight, but the Sheriff asked us to go with them to 459 Sycamore Street to pay Miss Sisstine Timpson a visit. I guess he thought this kind of news shouldn't wait until morning. Smelt agreed to ride with Beverly and me, and we followed the Sheriff's car to the home of Miss Sisstine Timpson.

"Who's there?" A lady's voice called cautiously from inside the door.

"Miss Timpson, it's the sheriff," was the reassuring reply. "There's an urgent matter that I think you should know about. We need to speak with you, please.

A streetlight shone brightly on our cars parked at the curb in front of the house, and the soft lights on either side of the door illuminated our faces as we stood waiting. Then we saw the curtain move slightly at the window and seconds later heard the thud of the tumblers as she turned the key in two locks. The young woman standing before us not only looked frightened as she gazed on our small entourage, she looked identical to Sissy Timpson, the sweet girl I had grown to call my sister.

The sheriff spoke calmly, introducing each of us and briefly stating the reason for our visit. He apologized for calling on her at this ungodly hour and without notice but, under the circumstances, he hoped she would understand and appreciate the magnitude of the visit. He asked if we might talk inside.

With a polite "Of course you may. Do come in," she opened the door wider.

There was softness in her voice that spoke kindness, politeness. We followed her lead through the dimly lit foyer and along a short hallway into the den that was modestly but tastefully decorated and smelled of apples and sweet spices. She nodded for us to sit and, without wasting time, the sheriff got right to the point of our visit.

Miss Timpson sat transfixed as I told the story of her sister Sisstine as I knew it and as Sissy had told it to me. Lucus Smelt added details and the sheriff added a few more. After hearing our story, Miss Timpson cried, thanking God and us for finding her sister.

I was still curious and found it impossible to wait until morning to call Sissy, so I called her right then.

It was now after 1:00 A.M. and Sissy's immediate thought was that something was wrong. I reassured her all was well. I just needed her to answer one question: Why didn't she ever tell me she had a twin sister?

"Well, I never thought it was important," she replied, "since she died when we were born."

Phew! Another shocker! I had to ask her to please repeat what she'd said—and she did, explaining she'd always been told her twin sister died at birth. This was making no sense!

I put Sissy on hold and turned to Missy asking where she was when Sissy lived at home. That was when we were introduced to the story as told by Misstine "Missy" Timpson, the identical twin sister of Sisstine "Sissy" Timpson. I listened intently as Missy told her story.

As payment for her mother's drug habit, Missy began, her mother gave her away to a crooked nurse at Grove General Hospital; Missy's poor dad never knew about her existence. By the time Missy learned about her father, he was already dead and she had no way of finding any living relatives. Of course, she thought Sissy was dead, too. Nurse Coats, as she was called, took Missy to Canada where she eventually left her in an orphanage.

Many years later, Nurse Coats wrote to Missy when Nurse Coats was dying of cancer.

In the letter, Missy said, Nurse Coats finally revealed that Missy was born in Grove, South Carolina. Missy said she found her way back to Grove a week after the twins' mother was murdered.

None of the locals ever questioned her, she said. They all just seemed happy to see her back in town and were overjoyed that she was not harmed. She soon realized they were thinking she was Sissy! So as not to further complicate things, Missy just pretended to be Sissy. Nobody ever asked her who she was, so she just let them go on with their case of misplaced identity.

Missy said she had also read many related articles about her family, and she reluctantly confessed that she was also "unsure" about Mr. Smelt. Missy glanced at Smelt, a look of apprehension on her face.

Missy, overcome with emotions, was again crying softly and dabbing her eyes with an embroidered linen handkerchief. Beverly was trying to calm her. I placed a consoling arm around Missy's shoulder as I went back to the phone where I had Sissy on hold. I took a deep breath and told Sissy the "whole" story. She could hardly believe what she was hearing. What a night!

When we all left Missy Timpson's, the night was far spent. Bev and I returned to the hotel, got a few hours of sleep, and were back in Glendale by noon on Friday; however, we were not alone. Traveling with us in our back seat was Sissy's look-alike.

That weekend's homecoming was one to remember. It was also a memorable time in Grove. Somehow the newspaper had gotten wind of the story and a front page story Friday morning read: *Sisters To Reunite After 28 Years*.

The best headline, however, was in the sports section in our local Glendale paper. The story told of a young man, Jason Marell Timpson, who was chosen in the first draft to play professionally for the Charlotte

Hornets.

Yes, some stories do have happy endings, and to this one there's yet more. Bev and I are expecting our first child in January. Missy now lives with Sissy and is employed as Sissy's personal secretary at *Timpson's Law Firm*. I keep in touch with Lucus Smelt, too, just for the heck of it all.

One thing more: That weekend we had baked chicken, potatoes, fresh asparagus with hollandaise sauce, fresh creamed corn, the best chocolate cake, and the sweetest tea in the state of North Carolina.

Yep! Grandma Shirl and Mama put on a cooking show!

INCREDULOUS

A WARM DECEMBER

I met him the first day he came to Clifton High as a new student. He had just moved to Landon the summer before his senior year. That was unusual. Most high school kids don't want to transfer to a new school their senior year, but Dra's parents loved him just that much and more. The New England area was too cold for his allergies, and a place like Landon was so southerly climate friendly.

He was tall, brown and drop dead gorgeous. I was very popular at Clifton, and I was an only child accustomed to getting everything I wanted. So here I was again telling Ben, my ex, to get lost. I wanted the new boy to be mine before he had a chance to look elsewhere.

That's exactly what happened: he became mine and we became inseparable.

Dra fell for me just as hard as I had fallen for him. Throughout our senior year, Dra and I were an item, and when the time came to vote for "Senior Superlatives" for our school annual, our classmates voted us the "handsomest couple."

We spent the last months of summer together as often as we could. We talked on the phone every day, but that was not the same as being with him. We talked about everything: college, cars, our families, relationship issues, our dreams, and the future. Marriage had been the deepest discussion of all. I loved Dra, and I loved being with Dra. He was very mannerly, mature, smart, and sincere; he, too, was an only child. There was only one thing about Dra that troubled me. Oftentimes, he acted worried and stressed; but then he would snap out of it, kiss me on the nose, and say that he was okay.

In late summer, we headed for different colleges that, gratefully, weren't too many miles apart. Our romance survived the transition. Dra accepted a football scholarship at Gam University in a neighboring county. Gam was highly recognized for its competitive sports program and championship teams.

On the other hand, I enrolled at Banker University, a school very near and dear to the hearts of my parents. I would have followed Dra to Gam, but I didn't have the heart to tell mom and dad I wouldn't be attending their alma mater. Understandably, Dra and I weren't able to see as much of each other once we started college, but we took advantage of the few opportunities we did have. I was able to get to a few of his home games, and we'd spent time together briefly during Thanksgiving break.

Now it was December 20, the last day of classes before Christmas vacation. The campus crowd was thinning fast as everyone was heading home for the holidays. I had finished the last of my first semester finals and was anxious to get home to my family and Dra. It was a warm winter day—strange within itself for a winter day to be so warm. My mama always said a warm Christmas makes for a fat grave. But it wasn't quite Christmas, yet.

I climbed into my red Corvette with its "DST 1913" plate on the front and fastened my seatbeat. I phoned Mom, as was the pattern. I told her I was about to leave and filled her in on my travel plans. Then I *texted* Dra that I would be at his dorm in an hour. Finally, I turned the key in the ignition and slipped into the heavy holiday traffic. I was already forty-five minutes late. I had to hurry!

I pulled onto Gam's campus slowing only at the speed bumps, trying hurriedly to get to Spencer Dorm where I'd hoped to see Dra standing with his bags, ready to jump in beside me; but he was not there as he had promised. I sounded the horn a couple of times thinking I would see him peek through the bright blue curtains of his upstairs window, but no luck. I waited a few minutes more and decided to go inside to see if he were waiting in the lobby; but to my surprise, the dorm master said he had already left with a couple of guys in an older model green Ford truck. I wondered who they could be since Dra knew I was coming to pick him up—even though I was a little late. Humph!

As I walked slowly back to the car, I heard it before I saw it: an old clunking sounding truck. Dra jumped out quickly, grabbed his bags from the back of his old hootie, and ran over to my car. He could tell I was a bit ticked off, but after he said he was sorry and kissed me on the nose, I forgot the whole thing. He never mentioned where he had been, or whom he was with. The two guys I'd seen in the old truck were strangers to me.

On the drive home, Dra seemed tired and sleepy, and when he did speak his words were slurred. More than once, I asked if he were okay and only once did he answer with an "Uh-uh-uh-okay." It was an hour's drive to his home. Thinking he was just exhausted from exams, I didn't disturb him with conversation, just listened to the radio and enjoyed our closeness. When I finally turned onto the long driveway at his home, I called his name and he awakened with a start. He told me to drive around back to the dirt road that led to the pond behind their house. How strange, but I did as he said. He dragged out slowly, his attention focused toward the pond.

I'd never before seen Dra looking this way. His face was flushed and his eyes red. He looked haggard. He walked laboriously in the direction of the pond, and as he turned back to me waving good-bye, I noticed for the first time the bruise on his face and the marks on his neck. "I'll call you later," was all that was said. He hefted the two heavy bags onto his shoulders and stumbled toward the pond. At the water's edge, he turned to me again, blew me a kiss, and jumped into the pond!

I can only remember my piercing screams, loud enough that his father heard and came running. I have no memory of the events that immediately followed, but Dra's father explained later that through my screaming and crying, I'd told him Dra had jumped into the pond. Dra's father did manage to pull him from the pond that warm winter day. The paramedics were there in a flash, and Dra's life was saved. Dra's father became a real-life hero that day.

I sat between Dra's mom and dad in a waiting room that was only steps from Dra's hospital room. My parents' demeanor as they sat adjacent to us showed great concern; they, too, were visibly upset. We were all in deep thought, wondering what, possibly, could have led to the near tragedy that had shaken us all to the core, but Dra had left in my car that day a major piece of the puzzle. My hands shook and my voice trembled as I shared the letter I'd found on the passenger seat of my car.

Dear Belinda,

I thought your love would overpower the life I lived in Vermont. I know I told you the reason we moved to N.C. was the climate and my allergies, but that wasn't quite the whole story.

I was in love with a girl named Fran. We were very close. To be perfectly honest,

Belinda, I never stopped loving her. Fran's parents were murdered and her brothers were worthless druggies who everyone suspected killed their parents. Fran and I made some mistakes: she got pregnant and I got into drugs. Yes, Belinda, the really heavy stuff.

One night, I was on one of my highs. With Fran by my side, I crashed my sports car into a barricade at the end of a road. She and the baby were killed instantly. I've paid my dues, though I got off light; but that's another story. Still I didn't think I would ever be sane again.
My parents thought it best that we leave the North and find a quiet southern town where I could start all over. This became something we would have to do over and over again.

I've been able to keep my grades up. Coupled with my skills in sports, I managed to get several great scholar-ship offers. Now with you in my life, I couldn't have asked for better. Then they started again—the calls and threats. They've found me again! Each time before, I had been lucky enough to escape them—Fran's brothers—the two dealers who'd turned me on to drugs then blamed me for Fran's death. They've found me again; called me last night on the dorms' hall phone.

They told me how easy it was to track me down using the internet and a little patience. They saw my picture with an internet college sports article. With that information in hand, it didn't take much to track me right to my dorm. I know it will only be a matter of time before they come for me.

Belinda, please understand: I am tired of running. Moving here was only the third time my parents have relocated to save me from them and another bout with addiction. I just can't do it anymore.

I managed to get this letter written while waiting for you to arrive, and—Oh no! They're here!

That was all he'd had time to write.

The arrival of two policemen interrupted our conversation. Among other things, the officers had come to tell my parents they'd been cleared and would not be charged with the deaths of the two fellows in the old green Ford truck that had veered into their path. Without going into great details, they also said blood evidence indicated both men were *under the influence* at the time of the accident.

When I hadn't arrived home within reasonable time and there was no response to their calls to my cell phone, Mom and Dad had become worried and had gone to search for me. Because they knew my travel plans and hadn't gotten an answer when they called Dra's parents, they decided to start at Dra's parents' home and travel my route all the way back to my dormitory.

Fortunately, a neighbor out walking her dogs saw my parents as they were leaving Dra's family's home; she told them about the event that had occurred earlier. My parents headed for the local hospital hoping they would find me there and that all was better than the neighbor had implied.

They were on a curvy road, almost at their turn onto the main highway, when an old green Ford truck came out of nowhere traveling left of the center line and too fast for conditions.

Dad swerved to avoid the truck. The guy driving the truck hit an embankment then ricocheted head-on into a tree. Both men in the truck were killed on impact.

Our fervent prayers were answered when we received word that Dra was awake and that we could visit him briefly. By ones and twos we went in to spend a couple of minutes with him; he recognized us all. Miraculously, Dra was eventually able to tell us his story.

He was standing outside his dorm waiting for me to pick him up for our trip home for the holidays. He was thinking back on our conversation the night before and decided to confess everything to me in a letter. He had almost finished writing the letter when the two brothers found him.

Dra's parents shared nightmarish tales a distraught Dra had told them of how Fran's brothers terrorized him and, more than once, the brothers had pulled a gun on Dra forcing him to use drugs. Dra's parents said they reported the incidents to authorities as soon as they learned of them, but the brothers seemed to be masters of illusion. The cops never found them until that fateful day.

All that was five years ago. My parents and Dra are receiving therapy for post traumatic stress disorder, but we're all doing well. I would like to think my love for each of them played some small part in their healing.

It's now Christmas Day, 2010, and Mr. and Mrs. AnDra Wesson are happily celebrating with our three month old son, AnDra Coda Wesson, Jr., at a ski resort in Vermont. Little AnDra's grandmothers are both in the kitchen cooking our favorite Christmas meal of duck with all the trimmings; his grandfathers, are watching a football game on TV. My mannerly, smart, mature husband is taking notes, since he is the best coach West Vermont High has ever had.

SPIRITUAL BLISS

I CONSIDER IT HOLY

Strange things do happen, but surely there's always some explanation. However, several really unusual things have happened to me—things for which I can't seem to find an explanation except that there is something religious in it, or from God. The event might come as a dream or an apparition, or strangers who become friends or strangers I never see again.

I recall a time when I was about seven years old. I'd been very sick all night. I was hot to the point of being feverish. I'd awakened drenched in sweat in the middle of a summer night. I wanted to call out for someone to help me; but everyone was fast asleep, and I was too weak to even move. My lips were moving, but no sound came out. After some time, I fell back to sleep and the next morning I awakened feeling no better.

My grandmother took one look at me and asked if I were okay. My parched lips muttered something that sounded less than a grunt. I had never had a fever, as best I could remember, and I had no idea what was wrong with me.

Grandmother walked out of the room. Then all of a sudden a figure appeared and looked me over. It was more ghostlike than it was invisible, and it didn't seem to have come to do me harm. Whatever it was, this presence, its power was unmistakable. It was so strong, so awesomely powerful, that as it stood there stark still, it seemed I could feel it drawing the sickness out of my body.

I closed my eyes fearing any minute its ghostly form would change to something frightening that I could actually see better—maybe something terrible that I would recognize. Surely, I didn't want to see it. I guess I wasn't supposed to see anything more frightening than what had already entered my room. I guess I wasn't supposed to see it because by the time my grandmother returned with medicine for me, the figure was gone, and I was better: no fever, no chills, nothing.

It was like I was never sick.

Now, what was that? To me, it was the power of God. Maybe the Holy Spirit Himself, an angel or something divine; but from that day forward, I've always considered it holy.

A few months ago, at the ripe age of 55, I had a similar experience. I had had two surgeries in my stomach area one month apart. My recuperation was going well. I was feeling fine but still needed lots of bed rest. One day as I lay resting in bed, I could feel that presence— the same presence that had visited me when I was seven years old; the same presence that had instantly restored me from sickness to health. This time, however, I didn't fear the presence as I did when I was a little girl. Instead, I embraced it. I was so happy that I started to cry and when I did, I was suddenly consumed with a feeling of the strongest love I could ever imagine.

This time, instead of closing my eyes tightly in fear, I kept them wide open but saw nothing out of the ordinary. Still I could feel the presence towering over me and hugging me ever so tightly. In that moment, in that hug, I felt the purest form of love! It was nothing like I'd ever experienced. In that moment, I knew I would be alright.

When I went for my next doctor's visit, the doctor

commented that I was really healing fast! Oh, my goodness. If he only knew!

The next morning, I woke to find my husband moving about our bedroom. He wakes every morning at 4:45 A.M. to walk at the local park not too far from our home. I lay there quietly thinking I should be going with him.

Well, maybe next month. More than that, I was thinking if only my stomach would heal even more within the next two weeks, I could go with him to Las Vegas.

He slipped quietly out of the bedroom and into the hallway. Then I heard the sound of the kitchen door close behind him. Through the blinds, I saw his van's lights blink and listened as he drove away. I turned onto my back and caught a glimpse of what I thought was smoke or something more like foam.

It glided into the bedroom from the hall, but for reasons I'll never know, I wasn't afraid. By the time it crossed my husband's side of the bed, it was misty. It hovered directly over my stomach. Then I felt it go into one side of my stomach and out the other. Let's just say this: In two weeks I was pain free and in Vegas with my husband.

Now what was that? To me, it was the power of God. Maybe the Holy Spirit Himself, an angel, or something divine; but from that day forward, I've always considered it holy.

There was yet another time. Right after I turned fifty, night driving became increasingly difficult for me. Now that was almost too much for me to accept. Through my eyes, night time was suddenly becoming darker than I'd ever known it to be. "What's up with that?" I asked myself, but just as quickly dismissed the question with an "Oh, well."

I had just reconnected with my sorority and our meetings were held in a neighboring city. I was certain I could drive to the meetings, but my husband kept suggesting that I should ride with one of my sorors who lived in our town. No. I wanted to be a big "old" girl. Besides, I wasn't blind; I was just having some difficulty seeing to drive at night. I had all the answers: If I wore my glasses when I was driving, …. If I left the meetings a little earlier, …. If I drove a little bit more slowly…. I went to bed that night anxiously anticipating our sorority meeting the next day.

All night long I dreamed of traveling. I found myself driving in strange and exotic places filled with all kinds of excitement, but I never could find my way back home. When I awakened the next morning I was a nervous wreck!

I went to my computer and pulled up *MapQuest* to get directions to the meeting place. I studied the map and read the directions. They were simple; no need to print. After exiting the main highway, there were only three or four turns and I'd be at the meeting site. Confident I could remember the few turns, I stood at the computer a couple minutes more reading the directions aloud and reciting them over and over until I had them memorized.

That afternoon, I set out for my meeting which was a forty-five minute drive according to MapQuest. It was a beautiful afternoon. Traffic wasn't too heavy, and soon I was deep in reminiscence and caught up in the sounds of the smooth jazz CD that was playing. As I rolled into the city where the meeting was scheduled, I suddenly realized I couldn't remember my first exit! I picked my brain, frantically trying to pull up any inkling of a clue.

Why, I could have kicked myself for not printing those directions! In retrospect, that would have been so easy, but at the moment that was out of the question.

Frustration began to set in. Then out of nowhere, like

a vision, I saw the word *Legend*. It really threw me for a loop. Actually, it startled me. "What is a 'legend'?" I asked myself. "What does this mean?"

I traveled about 5 miles further, and a billboard caught my attention. It advertised a golf tournament; but there, posted in giant letters on the advertisement, was the word "Legend." So as the sign on the billboard directed, I took the next right turn. Believe it or not, it was the exit I needed!

I remembered the next few turns and arrived at my destination safe and sound and with time to spare.

Now what was that? To me it was the power of God. Maybe the Holy Spirit Himself, an angel or something divine; but from that day forward, I've always considered it holy.

SACRED OMNIPOTENCE

HE CALLED ME DAUGHTER

My star, my hero, a wonder worker! I was so excited; my emotions so stirred that I could hardly sleep. I am his favorite fan, and he is coming to a nearby village near the harbor! Why was I still in bed? I had to stop this dreaming and soliloquizing.

I rushed my frail body as I hurriedly bathed in the old cracked porcelain basin. I slipped on my long brown dress and covered my head and both sides of my face with my clean, well worn, scarf. I had to carefully conceal myself from most of the town's people. I hurriedly ate a bit of breakfast comprised mainly of bread and a cup of cold goat's milk. I needed energy. I had a two mile walk from Capernaum, my small seaside village, to the Galilee seashore.

It was early morning when I started my journey. The sun was just starting to peak over the horizon. I walked a half-mile before I strolled past the house where Peter lodged. A fancy wooden ladder led up to the roof which was sometimes used as an outdoor room. "How modest," I thought. The roof was partly shaded by a matted superstructure. As I turned my attention from this fine home, I thought back on my humble tent. I could do better, but I needed to use my money otherwise. I needed it to get help for my terrible illness.

Walking further, I passed the tax offices where the soldiers were standing at their usual posts. I tried to walk faster, but the cramping pain and feeling of fullness wouldn't allow me to increase my pace very much. As I got closer to my destination I realized I wasn't so early after all. Some had evidently camped here overnight. I could hardly walk as I approached the area. The crowd was heavy and, not only was I tired from the walk, but my medical issue was bothering me tremendously. Only a miracle could help me.

People were everywhere! Men and women, young and old, boys and girls, mothers with babies. What a laity! Everyone loved this superstar and had come from far and wide to see him in the flesh right here in this small village. I had heard that in other towns some fans had passed out from the excitement of just getting a glimpse of him even before He started performing. They said his show was phenomenal! Some even declared he'd healed their hearts, minds, bodies and souls! What a man!

Through an opening in a tiny space between a man and his son, I caught a glimpse of the great man. He was coming in from the bright green boat that had just docked. His friends, about twelve of them, were with Him every step. He was wearing long, white, canonical attire with a gorgeous gold-fringed trim. His permanently tanned, flawless skin was glowing. He could hardly move for the crowd, but his friends protected Him like bodyguards on a mission.

I glanced in one direction and recognized Jarius, a fellow from the synagogue I used to attend before my illness. Jarius' young daughter was very sick. The star was really there to visit Jarius' home, but had stopped along the way.

I felt sorry for Jarius and his child. I knew all about suffering. I thought back on the last twelve years of my life. They'd been years filled with so much illness. Though I had seen many doctors, I continued to suffer a great deal under their care. I thought, too, of all the money I had spent trying to get well. Instead of getting better, I had actually become worse.

I really didn't want Jarius to see me, or anyone else who might recognize me. It was against the law for someone sick to be out and among the crowd. Everyone knew me as "the sick lady." No one wanted to be around me, so I usually stayed away from people. When I did have to venture out to the well or to the trade market, people called me ugly names: "unclean," "nasty," "impure," "diseased." They would move from the path when they saw me coming. They were so insensitive.

Jarius led most of the studies at the synagogue so he knew of my condition. He even agreed with the village tradition that barred me from being among others because of my condition.

They treated me like I was a contagious monster.

No one knew how badly this feeling of isolation hurt me. On this day—this one day out of twelve years—I wanted to forget my condition. I wanted to at least get a glimpse of this superstar. To do so, I had to forget tradition; and more than anything, I had faith. I had to forget my thoughts and press on toward the front of the crowd. He might never show in this area again, and I longed to at least see him.

Some of the people started to notice me. I could tell by their furrowed brows and concealed whispers. I was glad they moved farther away from me; it gave me a chance to inch a little closer toward the front of the crowd. Before I knew it, I was within a mere reach of the superstar we all had come to see.

Did I dare get closer? Suddenly I felt frigid and afraid, but a faithful force was gnawing at my heart and soul, and I was jolted by a thought. I didn't have to get all over him, all in his face to get his attention. Suppose I simply touched him.

My faith started to take control. "If I could just touch the fringe of his shawl in faith," I thought, "I would be made whole." With little apprehension, I reached out my frail fingers and gingerly touched the hem of his garment.

Straight away, the fountain of my blood dried up! Immediately I felt healed of my terrible infirmity. For twelve long agonizing years I had battled an issue of blood. I don't know how I was able to survive such a blood loss—why my blood supply was never completely depleted or sufficiently reduced to the point that I could no longer live.

Instantly my hero, my King of Kings, knew that virtue had gone out of him and turned asking, "Who touched me?"

Everything became still; there was silence all over the harbor. With so many people present, how could his bodyguards and friends know exactly who had touched his clothing? Still I trembled with fear and fell upon him confessing it was I. I was certain the hushed crowd was waiting for him to pronounce my death sentence. Instead, those close enough to hear listened in disbelief as he spoke to me: "Daughter, thy faith has made thee whole: go in peace, and be whole of thy plague."

I stared in awe. He'd called me 'Daughter!'
I did exactly as he'd directed. I did "go in peace" and I am "whole."

Hundreds must have touched Him, but I was the only one who derived benefit. Only I sought Him, Jesus, with a deep love in my soul and the faith that just to touch the hem of his garment would heal me forever.

FAMILIAR BELIEF

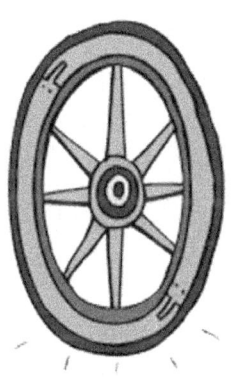

MY JOE: THE GREATEST LOVE STORY

At some time or other, every woman feels she has the best man in the world. What a great feeling! But, I tell you: No woman has ever had a man like my Joe! You must first know me in order to appreciate my Joe.

My name is Mar, at least that's what my Joe calls me. I'm a dark-haired, petite young woman standing a little taller than five feet. My dark, mysterious eyes are my best feature. When you look into them you see hope, understanding, and kindness; but when I look back through them, I only see him, Joe. To me, my Joe is the reason the sun rises and shines; the reason love songs are sung. My Joe is like the fragrant breath of spring and the cooling rains of summer. "There is no man mightier than my Joe," I would always say. Then my son came along. The whole world knows my son. With his arrival, the miracle I call life began to become difficult and unknowing, but oh so sweet.

Joe and I have known each other since childhood. We are both of Jewish decent and lived in a small village in Palestine. When I really noticed Joe, he was a young man. I took one look at him and my breath caught in my throat. I couldn't believe the change! He was tall, handsome, and strong; a builder who traveled to other towns to find work when there was no work for him to do in our village. Since Joe was so skilled at his craft, he had no problem finding something to hammer and nail.

In our culture, it was improper for a woman to make passes at a man, so surely you can imagine my elation when I realized Joe had begun to notice me. Over time, my father approved of Joe and allowed us to date, which was nothing more than chaperoned conversations. This went on for some time. Joe was a perfect gentleman—perfect and pure. He insisted that we remain chaste until we married which, of course, our culture expected of everyone who wasn't yet married.

During one of our many lengthy conversations, Joe told me he'd had no interest in me when we were playmates during our childhood years.

"I had no interest in girls at all," he'd added with a chuckle. "What little boy does? But little boys don't remain little boys," he said with a smile.

Then he told of a day I was out shopping with my family. We were walking past the carpentry shop his family owned when he happened to catch a glimpse of me. He said he recognized me only because I was with my parents whom he'd recognized right away. I think I flushed when he said he couldn't believe I was their "little girl," adding he couldn't believe how much I'd grown up and how beautiful I was. He admitted he'd fallen hopelessly in love with me that very moment.

In our country, marriages were "arranged," and Joe said he knew he had to find a way to make ours happen. That day soon came. Joe's father paid my father a visit and marriage, I learned not long after, was the topic of discussion. Following custom, Joe's father revealed to my father, he had selected me to be the bride for his beloved son, Joe. I could hardly believe the wonderful news!

Oh, was I happy! Some of my friends hated the grooms they'd been chosen to marry, but God shined on me in giving me Joe.

The traditional pre-wedding activities soon followed. Joe and I entered into our marriage contract. He promised to support me as his wife and in turn, I made known my dowry. Joe gave my family a gift of money which would ultimately belong to me. That one simple act changed my status: I was set free from my parents' household though I continued to live with them. Individually, Joe and I took the ritual immersion. Then came our betrothal ceremony which was followed by the designated year long period during which we were to prepare ourselves to enter into the marriage covenant.

It seemed the whole village came out for the ceremony. Joe and I stood side by side underneath a canopy and publicly announced our engagement. Then we exchanged gifts and shared a cup of wine to seal our engagement vows. Like every groom, Joe had to return to his home to fulfill his many obligations during our betrothal. However, just before he left at the end of the ceremony, Joe again pledged his love to me by giving me a special bridal gift. During our days of separation, it was to be a constant reminder that he loved me and was thinking of me and that he would return to make me his wife.

Being officially engaged, or betrothed, was almost the same as being married with two major exceptions: we could not live together, and our relationship had to remain chaste. Breaking a betrothal agreement could be done only by the husband, but divorcing me would be Joe's last worry if left entirely to me. I would never do anything to cause him to distrust me or love me less. During our long separation, Joe busied himself preparing our new home. I, too, had lots to do helping my parents with chores and preparing for my wedding day.

The days without Joe were bearable only because I had so many tasks to occupy my time. Often I was kept so busy that I was pretty worn out by nightfall. As time passed, I noticed a change in myself. I was tiring more easily and often napped during the day. By bedtime, I would crawl onto my mat, exhausted. Something strange was happening to me—strange and certainly unexpected. I learned I was pregnant!

How could it be and how would I tell Joe? There had to be some mistake because I had never slept with Joe or any man!

While I wrestled with these questions and pondered how to explain the unexplainable, Joe was wrestling with problems of his own. He sensed something was troubling me, but didn't pressure me to know what it was: one more reason I say he is the best man in the world. While grappling with trying to understand and cope with the changes I was going through, Joe began having visions and dreams. Through his prayers and his inner struggles, the quality that prevailed was not justice, but mercy.

I needed to get away to a place where I could think, so I went to spend three months with my cousin, Beth, who was such a good listener and always so loving and caring. Beth was many years older than my teen years but she, too, was pregnant. Matter of fact, she was so old people were talking about her, saying she was too old to be with child. However, if they really knew my cousin, they would have known how long she had prayed to God to give her a child and of her faith that God does answer prayer. However, it appeared the answer to this prayer Beth prayed had certainly been a long time coming.

Beth was really excited about her pregnancy. No sooner than I had arrived at her home, Beth grabbed her stomach as her baby leaped inside of her. Her excitement was beyond measure. The baby, she said, had never done that before. I remember thinking maybe her sweet unborn had sensed something just in me.

Beth told me of how God spoke to her in dreams.

That made me think of Joe—the dreams and visions he had been having lately, and how much I missed him. Listening to Beth share that God often spoke to her in dreams also caused me to remember a dream I'd had. In it an angel appeared telling me I had been chosen by God to be the mother of His Son. If anyone could understand my emotional turmoil, surely it was Beth, so I told her about my circumstances. Interestingly enough, she believed me. That's why I didn't mind traveling all those miles to visit Beth. I knew she would believe me and, being filled with the Holy Spirit, she said she knew immediately the words I had spoken were true.

Visiting Beth helped to bring a sense of calmness and acceptance of what was happening to me. The more I talked with and listened to God, the more things really started to come together. I know with God, all things are possible. I returned home happy and stress free for God had also spoken to me.

One spring day, Joe walked to my family's two-room cottage constructed of mud and bricks. He talked excitedly of our approaching wedding day and about his progress on the home we would soon share. Then, with great tenderness in his eyes and his voice, he reminded me how much he loved me. I couldn't bear to keep my secret from him any longer. Today had to be the day; so as we sat under a tree in my parents' yard, I sadly told Joe I was pregnant. I sought desperately to find the words to explain that I didn't understand how it was so since I had never been with a man. Joe was troubled, but his words were kind and gentle when he said he believed me and that we would work it out.

What manner of man would believe the woman to whom he is betrothed when she tells him she is pregnant but still chaste? Moreover, what does he think of her when he knows with no uncertainty that he is not the father of the child she is carrying? Well, my Joe believed me because, he said, this news had come to him in a dream but he thought it would be upsetting to me if he'd shared it with me. That's my Joe: the best man in the world.

The long period of our betrothal ended. I left my parents' home and joined Joe in our very own home. Joe was very protective of me now and sheltered me from the curious stares of the villagers and the gossip that was sure to come no sooner than they noticed my fullness and began to recount the time that had passed since my wedding day. Joe seemed to love me even more with each passing day. When my eyes questioned why, he'd tell me the same story: it was something about me, and the baby, and the inspirational and angelic dreams he'd been having. I finally shared with Joe my message from the angel. He simply smiled as he reached out and drew me closer to him.

I know it sounds so unlikely, but Joe and I didn't engage intimately after we were married, at least not until after the baby was born. Something in his dreams, he said, made him keep his distance.

One day the town was in an uproar. The emperor had issued an order: everyone had to return to the city of their birth to pay their taxes, about a four day journey for Joe. I was quite far along in my pregnancy, but Joe had no choice but to take me with him. What a journey!

I traveled almost all the way on the back of a little donkey with Joe walking close beside. How uncomfortable a ride; and before we arrived, I knew my time to deliver had come. Joe was anxious to get a room for us at an inn; but to our dismay, there were no vacancies to be found. My Joe pleaded our case to one innkeeper who finally offered us the last available place he had: shelter in a stable.

Joe helped me off the donkey and onto a bed of sweet-smelling hay where the miracle came to life.

My precious baby boy was born. I held him close finding it hard to believe I was really experiencing all the angel had told me. I swaddled the baby, and we laid him in an old livestock trough filled with fresh hay.

The animals were first to witness the miracle. A host of angels filled the skies singing songs of praises and great joy, and people began to arrive to see for themselves this miracle. Among them were wise men and kings who brought expensive gifts. Shepherds came though they weren't able to afford gifts for the baby. Still we welcomed them because in their hearts they brought a prayer.

We named the baby Jesus, the name given to me by the angel; and just as the angel had foretold, my Jesus did become the King of Kings, the Savior who took away the sins of the world. My baby was not just my miracle. He was the world's miracle.

There was never enough said about my Joe: his love for me and his love for the son he helped me bring up. That's why I share this story of our love. My Joe was really named Joseph—a powerful man, an obedient servant of God, and a considerate husband; the husband whose father chose me to be Joe's bride; the man who God made to love me.

In a quiet moment when I was alone with God, I asked Him, "Why an old stable?"

He replied, "Where would you expect a Lamb to be born?"

The rest of this story is Christmas.

SPIRITUAL REALITY

SUMMER OF THE DEER

Summer days, Hm-m-m, we loved and lived for them! That summer we died.

It was an implausible summer from the start.

The happiness of the last day of school usually lasted all summer, but that year I felt lonesome and melancholy the very next day. It was a feeling that something bad was going to come. The rhythm of my heart was sad, and too many times it seemed to skip a beat. That day, it was downright cold for a North Carolina summer: seventy-three degrees the lady on the radio said. Hm-m-m it just wasn't a normal summer from the start.

Ours was an all black neighborhood with a dusty, rocky strip for a road. We were poor sharecroppers; but when that's all you know, then it seems okay. We didn't even realize we were poor. For us, it as a way of life. The houses were clustered close together. After the seventh house, which was mine, the woods began. Across the strip of a road was an endless field of which an acre or more was a vegetable garden. Summers for us weren't all play. Even we kids had to work the vegetables in that field.

A white family owned the whole block: woods, field and all. So my next door neighbors to the left were the animals in the woods; to the right, an abandoned house. Those woods were also the war zone for the white hunters and the brown deer.

I was thinking about brown as I listened to the radio that crisp morning. There I was sitting on the porch eating cornflakes; wearing shorts, flip flops, and a sweater. Yes, brown—that skin color.

My two little brothers loved to play. All summer long they were running, catching, play fighting usually not wearing a shirt or shoes; but this morning they came outside wearing tan colored shorts and brown t-shirts with long sleeves. What a style for this summer of 1969. I wondered if every day would be this cool.

My brothers played all morning, running past me a dozen times or more. I was into "Didn't I Blow Your Mind This Time, Didn't I?" playing on the radio and daydreaming about him again. That's what teen girls do. It's perfectly normal. It was who I was daydreaming about that society would say wasn't normal.

I also remembered the white boys and men: a couple of them, and then more and more. They passed as I sat and watched. They were dressed in camouflage brown, going to the war zone to have it out with the deer family. I remember thinking, "Do they really need to kill those poor deer? I know they all have plenty of food."

Seems that my uncle could hear my thoughts as he came out the front screen door. Out of the blue he commented that hunting was a sport for them just like fishing was a sport for him.

I told him there was still something wrong: we needed the fish for food. Anyway, it wasn't hunting season.
My uncle said he had asked one of the younger boys, the one with the piercing blue eyes—the only one who would ever speak to us black folks—why they were hunting out of season.

I knew the one he was talking about; I even knew his

name. It was Ven. He told me secretly one hot summer night last year.

With his head down, my uncle said he would only tell me, "Try to keep those little brothers of yours from around these woods." He went on to say that some of those men wear white at night and don't only hunt deer. They claim they just want the skin and antlers. Suddenly I heard gunshots: I knew they'd already spotted deer.

That really was not all Ven told me last Fourth of July. When it's Independence Day in Hathfill, all of the people just become one and eat and play games and forget all about race. That's why I love that holiday most of all. That night, as the fireworks lit up the darkened sky, Ven told me for the first time that he loved me. I told him I loved him, too. This just couldn't happen to a couple from different races, not in the southern city of Hathfill in 1969. I secretly met him recently in the empty house next door, and we did more than talk. Now all I do is dream.

I stopped daydreaming and immediately turned to tell my brothers, Sammy and Glenn, to stay near the old wood pile on the other side of the shed, but they were nowhere in sight. Suddenly there were more shots in the woods. I started yelling, calling to my little brothers. Uncle Charles did, too. Then suddenly the boy with the piercing blues eyes came stumbling out of the woods with tears rolling down his face.

At first I thought he was talking out of his head as we stood face to face. He was going on and on about how he really liked black people and black people had never done anything to him; how he didn't want to go hunting. Through his sobs he mumbled a few more words, then I heard him say, "maybe dead." I was able to make out, "I stepped….and one got me. I will always love you. They …. not even in the woods …."

As the boys stood looking at them from the edge of the land we lived on, those men shot both of my brothers! The boys weren't even in the woods! My uncle and I took off to the edge of the yard where both boys had fallen. Then all the men came out of the woods and that's when everything started to happen so supernaturally fast.

Everyone, the blacks and whites—just as if it were Independence Day—started to gather. But everyone had to run; they had to scurry. I couldn't get to my brothers' lifeless bodies because the deer had gone wild, stomping and piercing. I looked back, and what I saw will forever be etched in my memory. The deer, hundreds of them, were stampeding. They were running and pounding the hunters and stepping on their guns. I stopped, but everyone else kept running.

My eyes fell on one deer, the only one that was white. I had never seen a white deer in my life, and that deer had blue eyes! It stood stark still and stared at me with its piercing blue eyes. I then saw Glenn and Sammy's lifeless forms on the ground. The white deer went over and licked my brothers' dead faces, and both rose up as if from a restful sleep. I went over and grabbed them by their hands, and they slowly opened their eyes and smiled. Sammy was the first to speak.

"Sissy, did you know there's a beautiful place where Ven lives?" he asked. "I think it's named after him. We went there."

Then Glenn joined in: "I think it's named after him, too, 'cause the sign on the gate read 'Welcome H-e-a-Ven.' The next thing I knew, we were back here with you, Sissy."

After the deer disappeared back into the woods and the injured were carried away in ambulances, some in cars driven by their loved ones, I saw my beloved Ven as the coroner covered his face.

That happened forty years ago. When my handsome

son with the piercing eyes and curly reddish-blond hair comes to visit me, he still loves to hear me tell this unbelievable story. He enjoys visiting me in the beautiful home we had built on the land in the same woods where the deer once lived—land that Ven's mother left in our name. She died from a broken heart two years after Ven. That same land now has signs that read: "No Hunting."

FAITHFULNESS

ENTRUST

To believe, to choose to stay with the plan:
To continue without knowing,
To feel invisible strength,
To know God's will in me,
To be, to become,
To heal, and tell.

When I surrendered all
He stepped out.
He led,
I followed.
And oh, what a path!
I crept,
crawled,
walked,

skipped,
ran!
I fell upon my knees and looked up.
His lips breathed life
Then whispered.
I listened
And smiled with chilled skin
and blushing cheeks.

Wait on Him; He is real!
A secret worth telling,
A song worth singing,
and a story be told.
He is real!

ABOUT THE AUTHOR

Regina Lindsey-Jenkins Emerson was born in Chatham County, North Carolina. Her desire to write came from listening to her grandmother, Rosa Lindsey, tell stories of her life in the rural towns and communities of Goldston, Bear Creek, Taylor's Chapel and Gulf in central North Carolina. Emerson is the oldest of six siblings. She graduated from Saint Augustine's College in Raleigh, North Carolina with a Bachelor of Arts degree in Education and has completed further studies at University of North Carolina at Chapel Hill.

Emerson, a retired elementary school teacher, enjoys: traveling, participating in church activities, reading and, of course, writing. She has two adult children, Nikki and Jamie; and a stepson, Levern. She is a member of many organizations and says her sorority, Delta Sigma Theta, is her favorite way to participate in community activities.

Emerson lives in Sanford, North Carolina. She now spends most of days simply enjoying life with her husband, James, also a retired educator, their children and five grandchildren: April, Nathan, Jasney, Hailey and Kierra.